Walt Disney's

Swiss Family Robinson

Senior Designer: Elaine Lopez
Editor: Sharon Fass Yates
Editorial Director: Pamela Pia

Walt Disney's Swiss Family Robinson copyright © 1956, 2006 Disney Enterprises, Inc.
Story adapted by Jean Lewis from the book by Johann Wyss. Illustrations by Paul Granger.

Copyright ©2008 Disney Enterprises, Inc. All Rights Reserved.
Published by Reader's Digest Children's Books,
Reader's Digest Road, Pleasantville, NY U.S.A. 10570-7000
and Reader's Digest Children's Publishing Limited,
The Ice House, 124-126 Walcot Street, Bath UK BA1 5BG
Reader's Digest Children's Books, the Pegasus logo,
and Reader's Digest are all registered trademarks of
The Reader's Digest Association, Inc. Manufactured in China.
1 3 5 7 9 10 8 6 4 2

Walt Disney's
Swiss Family Robinson

Illustrated by The Walt Disney Studios

Illustrations by Paul Granger

Story adapted by Jean Lewis from the book by Johann Wyss

Reader's Digest
Children's Books™

Pleasantville, New York • Montréal, Québec • Bath, United Kingdom

"Being shipwrecked is fun," yelled Francis, as he slid down the slippery deck.

His mother shuddered. Only the day before, the family had been snug and safe on the ship that was carrying them to a new home.

But then came the storm. The ship had run aground on the rocks. And now the Swiss family was alone on the shipwrecked vessel.

"Our only hope is that island," said the father. "We must build a raft and get to it."

"Perhaps we'll find buried treasure," said Ernst hopefully. "And pirates," added Francis.

The father and his two elder sons, Fritz and Ernst, set to work.

At last the raft was ready.

"Now, tie the animals so that they will float along behind us," said the father.

"Can chickens and that cow and pig swim?" asked Francis.

"These empty kegs will float in the water and hold them up," explained Fritz.

Ernst grinned. "I'll bet we're the first castaways to land with our own fresh milk and egg supply!"

"Don't forget Duke and Turk!" said Francis. The two big dogs wagged their tails. They were ready to leap aboard the raft. "No!" said the father. "The family first, then the things we really need. After that we'll see about the dogs."

But Francis had other ideas. When his father turned away, Francis quietly beckoned the dogs.

They swam after the raft, and when the Swiss family landed on the island, the two big dogs were with them.

It was a beautiful island.

"See," said Fritz, "the sand is as white as the snow at home."

"Oh, there are monkeys, too!" said Francis. "I'll have a monkey for a pet!"

"Look at those big coconut palms!" said Ernst.

"And here," said the father, "is a big tree to shelter us from the rain and wind—"

"—and from wild animals," added the mother.

The father, Fritz and Ernst set to work to build a tree house, high in the thick branches.

They made many trips to the wrecked ship, for they needed planks and nails and tools.

"Getting these heavy planks up into the tree is the hardest part," said Fritz.

His father nodded. "The house will take longer to build than I thought."

"What we need is an elephant," said Francis. "They're very strong."

The others laughed.

When part of the flooring was finished, Francis was allowed
to climb up.

"But just to make sure you don't fall—we'll tie this rope
around your waist," said Ernst.

They tied the other end to a strong branch.

"Now I can catch my monkey," said Francis. There were many monkeys in the branches. His father and brothers were too busy to notice him crawl out on a branch. Near the end sat a solemn-faced little monkey with big brown eyes.

"Here, monk. Here, monk," called Francis.

But the monkey backed away.

Francis followed, reaching for the monkey's paw. Then the animal suddenly screeched and swung by his tail to another branch.

Francis was so startled, he fell off!

The rope around his waist stopped him a foot or two above the ground.

"Francis, Francis, are you all right?"

His mother ran to him as Ernst cut the rope at the top. Francis jumped to the ground.

"No more tree climbing for you till the house is finished," said his mother.

Bored and unhappy and munching on a stick of sugar cane, Francis wandered off into the jungle.

He came to a wide clearing, and suddenly he stopped. There, nibbling on some young branches, stood a baby elephant!

Francis moved a little closer.

"Here, little elephant," cooed Francis.

He held out his stick of sugar cane and the elephant stretched out his trunk.

Carefully Francis untied the rope from around his waist and made a noose. The elephant stepped into the noose and Francis yanked it tight.

"Oh," said Francis happily. "I never knew anyone who had a baby elephant for a pet!"

Suddenly the elephant trumpeted shrilly and tried to free himself.

It was then that Francis saw the tiger. The big beast was crouching in the bushes, ready to spring.

"Go away! Scat!" yelled Francis. He picked up a rock and threw it.

At that moment the two big dogs, Duke and Turk, burst into the clearing. Behind them came Francis' mother. She clung tightly to Francis as the big dogs went for the tiger.

Outnumbered, the big cat shook himself free of the dogs and disappeared into the jungle.

"Oh, you wonderful, wonderful dogs!" said the mother, hugging them.

"They sure showed that old tiger who was boss!" said Francis proudly.

"Francis," said his mother sternly, "you might have been killed, wandering off like that!"

Francis hung his head. "I'm sorry, Mother. I didn't mean to scare you. But—" He looked longingly at the elephant. "But—please, couldn't I keep him now?"

His mother sighed. "All right, Francis," she said. "If you promise to look after him yourself."

"Oh boy!" yelped Francis. "A real elephant of my very own!"

Proudly he led the elephant back to where his father was building the tree house.

"Look, Father, I found an elephant to help us build the tree house!"

The father smiled and went back to hauling planks with Fritz and Ernst.

Francis stood close to the elephant's big ear. "It's a game," he whispered. "You pick up that plank, and then I'll give you some sugar cane."

And everyone but Francis was amazed to see the elephant raise a heavy plank high in the air.

"See?" said Francis proudly. "Just what we needed—an elephant!"

After that, Francis and his elephant were allowed to help build the tree house.

The elephant hauled the heavy planks up from the beach.

And when work was over for the day, he let Francis and his brothers ride on his back.

When the tree house was finished, the family gave a party. The elephant was guest of honor.

"For without Francis and his elephant," said the father, "our new home might never have been built."

The elephant raised his trunk, as though to say, "Thank you."

Then Francis proudly gave his elephant the sweetest and best sugar canes he could find.